Rose's Collage

Poetry by Christa Laririt

with illustrations by Susanna Liebow

ⓒB Calliope Books

Santa Barbara, CA

First Printing May 2003

Printed in the United States of America

Copyright © 2003 Christa Laririt

ISBN 0-9729106-0-3

LCCN 2003091852

Graphic design and typesetting by Bo Criss
bocrissdesign@hotmail.com

Proofreading by A. J. Sobczak
asobczak@ix.netcom.com

Website design by Loren Saunders
loren_saunders@hotmail.com

Cover art by Christa Laririt
Inside illustrations by Susanna Liebow
Author photo by Sebbastion Liebow

Calliope Books
PO Box 6223
Santa Barbara, CA 93160
www.calliopebooks.com
calliopebooks@hotmail.com

Acknowledgements

In reflection of those who helped make *Rose's Collage* come to light, all who I have made contact with play a part. All the friends, family, angels, and tricksters are here for a reason. Now I am able to enter new stages of my being, just as I help others into theirs. As Alfred, Lord Tennyson wrote:

> *I am a part of all that I have met;*
> *Yet all experience is an arch wherethrough*
> *Gleams that untravel'd world, whose margin fades*
> *For ever and for ever when I move.*

This book is possible because of the many beautiful souls whom I communicated with at one point or another during and prior to the five years it took to write. Even those who seemed more damaging at the time were really there challenging me to overcome obstacles within myself in order to be who I am now.

In the attic of the Free Methodist Church in Redmond, Oregon, I was part of a group of young teenagers who were asked what we most wanted to do in life. Seems like a simple and commonly asked question. At the time, I was in a deep depression due to divorce in my family; yet a quiet inner fire spoke up and said, "I am going to write a book about my life." Little did I know that the events filling the book were just beginning. In hope, I wavered on the emotional waters of life while looking through an arch of the untraveled world. I think that space is called NOW for here I am, still. Having written and published a novel in poetry, there are other works patiently waiting, sitting until it is their time to be rewritten. The arch entrance of the untraveled world widens. The more I do and become, the more possibilities open up. Certainly, I could not do any of this without so many of you. For support and encouragement in my early writing days, I will forever remember Rachael Jarvis, Jamie Lockwood, Rachel Kamperman, Carla Elise Fishman, Matthew Hogan, Bob Evans, Greg Lyons, Carol Chaete, and William Manly.

Publishing an early version of *Rose's Collage* was tempting but it wasn't until recently that I made contact with certain people who became part of this process. Sebbastion Liebow offered feedback with rewriting, beginning with reading the entire work at the library the day after I met him. Jina Carvalho of The Glendon Association is my mentor in book publishing and promotion. At a writing group, I met professional proofreader A. J. Sobczak. Bo Criss, graphic artist, paragliding instructor, and neighbor, helped the book take flight in print. Sitting next to me on the steps of Vedanta Temple looking out over the Pacific Ocean on Sundays is Susanna Liebow. We scribble in our journals. One Sunday, I said, "You ought to do something with all those divine drawings." So she did.

Rather than systems and institutions, people and life itself are educators. Within the institutions, however, I found many great and inspiring educators. We met at Mountain View High School and at Central Oregon Community College, both in Bend. We met at Simmons College in Boston. We are even family. Janice Rank and Jack Mitchell, I thank you for all the gifts of books over the years, even though the post office had to forward most of them to my next address. For teaching me to work hard, for strength, for support, for prayers, for love, I thank my parents, Jerry Rank and Lori Browning. For sibling rivalry, unconditional support, and always making sure I have a good sound system in my truck, I thank my brother, Tim Rank. Loren Saunders, I treasure our continuing correspondence and opportunities to learn with you.

Upon asking for healing, I became simultaneously involved with Clackamas Women's Services Domestic Violence Shelter and Poekoelan Tjimindi Tulen martial art at One With Heart in Portland, Oregon. These two places balanced one another in the process of turning me inside out and upside down. So many of you are still a part of me – Poekoelan practitioners who have been in my dreams are Guru Barbara Nagel, Pendekkar Janessa, Pendekkar Scott, Mas Eric, and Mas Sandy. From Clackamas Women's Services, I appreciated special friendships with Shannon Morris and Lois Daley-Kilcrease. Rose, wherever you are, I hope you know the value of your collage. May we help one another along the way to realize that we are all capable of walking on fire.

My work has appeared in the following places:

- "Corn Stalks" published in *The Cascade Reader*, an Oregon Journal, Spring 2002

- Cover of *Rose's Collage* featured at *The Power of Women* art exhibit, Women's Center Art Gallery, University of California, Santa Barbara, January-March 2003

- "All of Life is a Training Ground" voiced in *Homage on the Hill*, a film production by Art Spots Media in Seattle, February 2003, this poem to be included in the next collection

Poet's Statement
by Christa Laririt

My work is about awakening choices and about keeping a promise. It questions reality, as if someday we may all see more than just shadows on a cave wall.

In our world of chaos, I work to expose new perceptions, to relate what a few already know just by breathing. In order to communicate the vision of this transcendence, I give observations. These are a few frightening things and a few beautiful charms about the labyrinth of life.

This compilation is my version of transforming personal experience into timeless mythology, like a river that rumbles, then rests serenely. My story comes from a place of deep inner stirring. Through tangible poetry, I reconcile with madness that might otherwise claim a person in the midst of domestic violence. These increasing artistic moments of uniting heart, mind, body, and spirit are like musical notes that forever remain as expressed energy. Sometimes it even seems as though everything that exists has wild eyes. I work with the intention of becoming more aligned with the spiritual self in order to share the experience and connect others to a deeper level of life within themselves.

Rose's Collage is a dance, an appreciation of those who went before us, a continuation of the artistic currents of the Universe, and about hope, because we have to believe. We have to really believe.

Artist's Statement
by Susanna Liebow

My artwork is inspired by the multitudes of mental, emotional, physical, and spiritual experiences that compose my life. The expression of my experiences fluctuates between writing and drawing. Writing when my intellectual brain seeks expression. Drawing when my intellectual brain is too overwhelmed to find words that adequately display my state of mind.

Much of my artwork is conceived on the steps of the Vedanta Temple overlooking Santa Barbara, a place I frequently visit to clear my mind through the movement of my pen and the silence of the space.

It was a surprise and an honor to be acknowledged and asked to contribute to a work of art such as Christa Laririt has composed. I am thrilled to have the opportunity to share my own form of expression and of course, belief, in myself as well as the world around me.

Dedicated to those who inspire me
and to those who read this
and are inspired by it

Dedicated especially to
my first reader,
Sebbastion

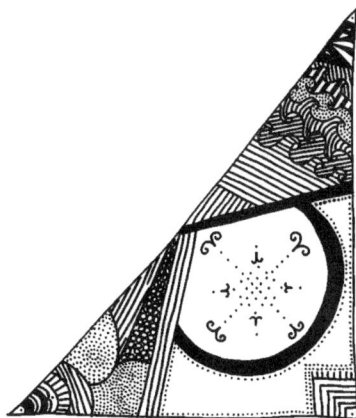

The Poems

Part 1
Setting up the Stage

Part II
Journey into the Labyrinth

Part III
Echo of the Spiral

Part 1

Setting up the Stage

Her Story: Part 1

She stands with hands
On hips and head high.
One foot is on a stack of books.
Lives and letters of others
Help her on her journey.
Her breasts point across land,
Climb mountains,
Grace
Across waters and seas.
She is a black silhouette.
Her feet are shaped
Into question marks.
There is so much
She wants to unravel.
Where
Will she go next?

Her Story: Part II

It is only a matter of time
Before she goes completely inside her head.
No thoughts.
Only existence.
Rush rush rush
In synchronicity with gravity
Move water particles
In the fountain
Leaving all other sounds
To their own drum beat.
Standing straight as an arrow
She links Heaven and Earth,
Is a medium between the two
As if they could not
Communicate without her.
Or perhaps she could not
Communicate with either of them
If she did not stand here
To take in the moment
Lasting for a lifetime.

Another misprint in the paper
Changes the fate of her evening
And possibly her life.
A door closes.
A door opens.
She moves in a direction
In this world where it seems
Fate is a huge house of ghosts.
At night they invade her dreams
But she wakes to interpret them
With the small fraction of her brain
That escaped atrophy.
She could stand straight
As an arrow and sing
With her diaphragm and sing
With her mouth and sing
With her soul but the door
Closed her out of that room by a simple
Misprint of a schedule.
Words change her life again.
Perhaps the ghosts will offer
A hint during evening rendezvous.
Day dances into night
Because the sun says hello
To the opposite hemisphere.
Stars say hello to her
And twinkle their time in eternity
While she writes her story.

Corn Stalks

Slowly they grow.
Corn stalks stretch tall
Behind the shorter vegetables.
Roots plunge
Into the core of Earth
With weeds in between rows
Beckoning me to feel soil
With hands, fingers, and toes.
I am tempted by a mud bath
With a view of the valley
Where Burlington Northern train
Cuts through signaling
Its passage then a wave of the hand
With a toot and a wave of the tail.
There are no doors or windows
Here to bar you out.
Space is free as wind making its dance
Like Chianti wine through my veins.
This is the juice of the gods.
Corn stalks stretch tall
Behind a bed of flowers
With leaves for tassels to line a garden
Of nutrition and health watered by
The Crooked River Fountain,
Photosynthesized by the Western Sun
And tendered by the hand.
They evolve with no special tricks for show.
Maize mixes in a collage of color
With backdrops of enormous day blue
And kisses of rain with passing clouds.
Sunset orange peeks up from Smith Rocks
Peeks up just before
Dusk gray night rendezvous
Tucks in the velvet hours layer by layer
And offers freedom to the moon
Curiously conversing with herself.

The Ditch Riders

Soda cans bounce off tools
On the truck's floorboard.
They clang and roll and shift with the driver.
Country hits proclaim honky-tonks
Of love, struggle, and summertime blues.
Road dust seeps through cracked windows
And circulates through the cab.
A pine tree air freshener
Dangles from the rear-view mirror.
Nostrils become coated with dust and pine.
The gray Chevy (with both doors dented
From cows leaning against them)
Rumbles along.
To the right is light flowing water.
To the left is range land.
Before us lies the road.

Abandoned trailers and cars
And garbage compiled and heaped
Forms a junkyard. I recognize
Toys I played with as a child
And I recognize several appliances.
All that we once desired in stores ends up here.
There is a woman standing there, too
In the middle
Of what we thought of as abandonment.
She leans against the doorway of a trailer
Watching us watch her
As we pass through her yard.
Curlers bind her hair.
A flowered nightgown hangs
From her body, moving
With the light afternoon breeze.

On the plateau rim canal road
Just above the gravel pit, we travel.
Today we are the ditch riders
Looking for signs and clues

That our lost bull was here.
We watch for a large hoofed trail
   Crossing the canal or pausing for a drink
    Under a dehydrating sun.
  Water rushes and swooshes
Through the canal. Perhaps the bull went,
   Instead, for a broken-down fence
    And left behind
  Barbed wire knots of fur.
All around is Juniper and Sagebrush.
   Has the bull gone
    For homeland or new land?

  We are the ditch riders
Traveling between where the bull came from
   And where it might be headed.
    We trail between land and water
   Looking both directions
For signs of animal passage.
   We trail toward destinations
    And move through perspectives.

Fertilizer

Thumbs hitch into back pockets of Wranglers.
Squinting eyes and one leather boot
      Are on a weathered board fence
We are about to tear down.
      My father mimics his father's stance
And I mimic my father's stance, too.
      Then father climbs into the Cat,
Fills its mouth with manure fertilizer,
      And transports it in a belly dump trailer.
I recycle every experience,
      Am mesmerized at how time
Turns everything upside down
      And disperses it across the land.

Later I watch my father
Scoop dirt and turn over the junk pile
      Easily like a midnight spoon
Into his favorite ice cream.
      He pulls levers while sitting
In his tractor seat
      In this valley while I watch
Chicken wire and rusted car parts,
      Milk and medicine bottles
Purpled and greened and soil soaked
      Reveal themselves as hints of history.
We place the bottles side by side
      In our kitchen window sill
To catch the daily sun and witness a new era,
      To inspire stories and smiles,
To remove the wall between
      The indoor and outdoor worlds.

Irrigating

Here I am again . . .
Driving down the cliff past the gravel pit
      To watch the textured valley open
            Between plateaus.
      Through time, land evolves
And so do we.
      Through time, land revitalizes
            And so can we.

      I wade through fields of alfalfa
And move wheel lines twice a day.
      Each motor is handled a bit
            Differently than the others.
      Do I turn on the gas?
Bang my hand against the starter box?
      Where is my crescent wrench?
            Am I strong enough?

      I crouch in the field, hysterical
That I thought I might be as competent
      As my 13-year-old self.
            Next to a main line valve, feet sink
      In mud after a 12-hour sprinkler rotation.
My heavy shoes remain buried in this mud
      While I run off with a crescent wrench
            And an empty soda can.

      I run because I must know
This land barefoot if I am to help it
      Become alfalfa and orchard grass.
            I run toward sunset.
      I run away from so many memories
Even when only the ghosts remain.
      I run barefooted because
            I have no rubber boots.

      The river calls me and I shed
Clothing of the day and drift with a slow current.
      The Crooked River changes
            Its shape as often as I come here.
      In this river, horses might pause,
Splash with hooves and make waves.
      Our horses might wade through water
            And wade through alfalfa.

In water I splash, make waves,
Then rise to cross fields and remember a day
When my brother and I moved wheel lines
Four turns across the field.
We laughed at ourselves for irrigating
Because we believed on that very day that the sun
Would turn blood red and we would disappear.
The evangelist predicted it so.

Yet we still moved forward,
Wading through alfalfa and laughing at ourselves
As we changed sprinklers again
The next morning.
Summers later I wade through fields,
Invite the refreshing mist of river,
And move forward across
The land of fertility.

My Father's House

Entering my father's house
Is like entering compartments of the mind
With furniture and books,
With tool boxes and overalls,
With plants and a toilet,
With tales of old and Do you remembers?
With skulls, agates, and feathers,
With old guns and old coins.

Bees buzz around the bathroom.
They seem frustrated by walls
And deceptive glass windows.
It often seems more practical
To use the Restroom of the Woods
Under an infinite sky while watching crickets
Dance in the climate
Of their breeding ground
Than to place one's bum
On a porcelain seat where bees buzzing
Look for an outlet
On which to vent a stinger.

The house is always in repair.
Only the deepest pressing issue
Receives its due attention—
A crack above a door
Through which mosquitoes and bees travel,
Shingles to replace the tin roof pitter-patter under rain,
A slanted floor settling into the valley,
Or a long-awaited door
On the bathroom that faces toward
The driveway so that at nighttime
When hues of blues turn into blacks
And twinkle twinkle little stars
Shine with all their might,
Headlights reveal all bathroom action.
I dart off through
The doorless way.

Among the repairs
In between layers of sheetrock
We tore down
Was a 1906 issue
Of *The Woman's Magazine*
Which sold for a cent.
On the cover
Is a woman
Feeding a horse from her hand.
Autumn leaves fall all around.
On the back page,
"Feminine Philosophy"
Offers resourceful advice—
"A woman can use
A hairpin for everything except
Keeping the children quiet."

Train to Ontario

At one time my uncle, the backwoodsman,
Wrote and was selected to travel by train to Ontario.
            Perhaps he wrote of Grandfather's migration
                        From Norway in 1919, when he crossed
            The Atlantic Ocean and traveled by train to Bashaw.
While camping one evening, he woke from the shaking Earth.
            Grandfather scrambled around inside in a collapsing tent
                        Like a wild animal caught in an unforgiving net
            Until he escaped and saw the red tail light
Of a caboose from a freight train
            Disappearing down the tracks.
                        He thought it was a bear.

            Perhaps he wrote of his mother wrestling with her sister
In the garden about who would put a dirty carrot
            In whose mouth and how Grandfather
                        Watched from the hill, laughing.
            Perhaps he wrote of Grandfather's garage
With stacks of lumber, barrels, compartments,
            And things put just so. He was a carpenter
                        Making this and repairing that.
            Just to the right of the garage door
Was a mounted mirror. A black comb lay on a nearby shelf.
            Grandfather wanted to look nice for the lady
                        When he went in for dinner.

            Perhaps, even in his early days,
He wrote of his isolation as he did years later:
            "At times I feel like Robinson Crusoe
                        On his island . . .
            Daniel Defoe wrote the book
Shortly after a real occurrence
            Of a man left for four years
                        On an island off Chile.
            He tamed the cats
To protect him from the rats and said
            They lay about him by the hundreds
                        And preserved him from the enemy."

Perhaps he wrote about composting
To fertilize the soil, remembering to daily thank the Lord
For his blessings, and living close to other animals,
Regardless of what people would say about his sanity.
Perhaps the backwoodsman wrote of things
No one will know except other students on the train to Ontario
Who waited extra long for him every time the train paused
And he stepped off to explore.
I wonder if they laughed with wide grins
When he returned from peeking between cars
With a face charcoaled black from smoke
Just as he laughed in the mirror at himself.

Bird Watching

This garden of vine and health
Is a fitting place for bird life
And human life gathering
In celebration of marriage.
Hearts point toward
One another so that fulfilling fate
Is a blessing multiplying
Into blessings.

Finches and plovers
In their chirpy flighty life
Of eating and bathing
And laying and mating
Watch friends and relatives
Visit during the tea party
Accompanied by lemon
And mint squares.

Tradition here meant that
We would play tennis
Except my shoes were left in
My truck parked at
A friend's house back in the USA
Along with my blue Gap hat that
I thought was lost
In the basement.

Instead, we are bird watchers
With binoculars and Audubon books
At Chaplin, a sodium sulfate mine
From which we get detergent,
Textile dye, paper, and mineral feeds.
These inland lakes are inhabited
By migrating shorebirds traveling
Between Alaska and South America.

From these waters come brine shrimp.
Hundreds of eggs we barely see
Sit on my fingertip after I brushed
The brown shore
To take a closer look
At life swimming and fluttering
Through the food chain
Ecosystem of time.

Melting glaciers created
Prairie potholes. Wetlands scattered
Across the plains of Canada
Providing resting places
For migratory birds during flights.
Here we find Piping Plovers,
Sanderlings, Sandpipers,
Godwits, and Willets.

Birds communicate through calls
Whistling, singing, and squawking.
They drive off intruders,
Instruct chicks, and mate.
They feed in groups,
Dig their bills in mud,
Or hunt on sight by pausing
Then racing.

An Avocet puts on a show for guests.
She is a charmer with her long legs,
Brilliant rusty orange neck,
And long bill tipping upward.
She runs in front of us,
Lifts black and blue striped wings wide,
And beckons us to trail her.
We do. Her nest is protected.

Skies are vast and lakes are wide,
Providing habitat for many creatures.
Between prairies of clover
We drive on a dirt road.
Between shallow lakes
It appears that long-legged
American Avocets and Willets
Are walking on water.

Indeed this is a holy place,
A sanctuary in the land of living skies.
Here in Saskatchewan the Sun
Breaks through clouds.
Rays cascade down
Through blue skies touching Earth
Like blessings and kisses
On sparkling silver lakes.

Balderdash

It is as if our lives
Are a game of Balderdash
        Where each player writes a definition.
                Oohs and aahs,
        Laughs and cries
Come from those around us.
        We learn from each other,
                Do best
        When everyone participates
Like the preparation of a turkey dinner.
        Family members join together
                Who are otherwise
        Countries apart.
A game of Balderdash
        Means a word such as peridontiphile
                Can be defined as anything—
Distilled water used to rub a bruise,
The accumulating scum underneath a whaling ship,
        The study of ticket stubs,
                A salad containing head cheese,
        A musician of cheeks
Who plays the theme from *The Lone Ranger*
        Or someone fully involved in books who is
                Unaware of the events of the world.

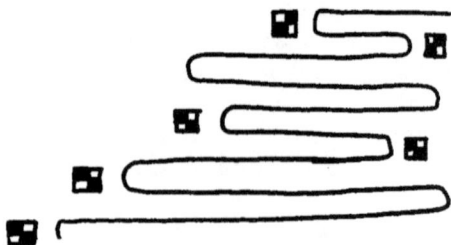

The Hum of Light

For half of time,
Blending with civilization
Moves body and mind
Into a quiet life of desperation.

I heard that madness begins
Once we realize the absurdities
Surrounding us.
Then it just grows.

I have seen swallows and swans
Through binoculars like superhuman eyes,
Have even bumped into windows
With curious watching to be nearer,

Nearer to that kind of life so I identify
Migrating patterns, summer and winter grounds.
Brown streaks blacken into maturity.
Yellow and orange hues attract mates.

I see subdivisions disappear
While flying higher in the airplane
For my travels with an itch under my foot
And itches at the ends of fingers.

My meal is V-8 and an apple.
At times like these
I apply more thought to words.
My hunger is not for food or wealth.

It is for wood between fingers.
It is for an infinite sky.
It is for the remaining words
Which great lovers exchange.

Back and Forth

Back and forth.
Back and forth.
I wander on a winding road
Between houses
Wandering
Through a nocturnal landscape.
Light seeps through windows
Out of blackened shacks.
Grayed skies loom
Beyond the blowing trees
With leaves gravitated toward roots,
With leaves ragged like my pajamas,
With leaves ragged like
My weathered hair wavering
As I lean forward
Into wind direction
Holding a hat down on my head.
I wonder if I might lose both.
Back and forth.
Back and forth.
I wander on a winding road
Between houses.

For the Lost Poems

Containing creatures all about
With sly eyes and wide tangled smiles

Containing a giant dirty snowman
Wearing my grandmother's red bead necklace

Containing silly love songs written
On miniature tablets during long road trips

Containing songs for my father
So he could hear them when he drove the tractor

Containing an old bicycle from the garage
Venturing unstoppable into the rain

Containing horses tied up in fields
Held back from galloping and kicking

Containing snakes under the porch
And snakes in the middle of the road

Containing a wolf in the yard
Watching us during night arrival

Containing agates on a winding path
To an abandoned farmhouse of treasures

Containing Rajneeshpuram
Turning Antelope into a ghost town

Containing calves suckling fingers
While they lie on doormats like dogs

Containing a spunky cow dog
That kept getting hit by the cars it bit

Containing a coffin containing
My mother's infant son

Containing a bawling Holstein calf
On the highway beside its dead mother

Containing burning kitchens
And vehement screaming in the night

Containing carousel horses
And cold morning glances

Containing the cut up pieces
Of my torso plastered on a canvas

Containing all the old men
Who tried to take my naïve hand

Containing serious letters written
To God, to Satan, to the devils in my closet

Containing hurried supermarket shoppers
In their quest for security and salvation

Containing all the ways of coloring
Outside the lines at church camps

Containing bats in the church at midnight
After stories of the Jim Jones Tragedy

Containing films on the mark of the beast
Where the last Christians are decapitated

Containing the drawings of heavy crosses
And the burning of a broken heart

Containing the sexual identity dilemma
Belonging to so many of us

Containing violent temptations of mine
And suicidal attempts by friends

Containing a perplexing fascination
Of the personal lives of criminals

Containing dreams of my Alcatraz imprisonment
Before I knew the place existed

Containing casual conversations
Of one asylum patient with another

Containing contradictions
In words that no one understands

Containing pale faces gracefully
Losing brown leaves to walk in snow

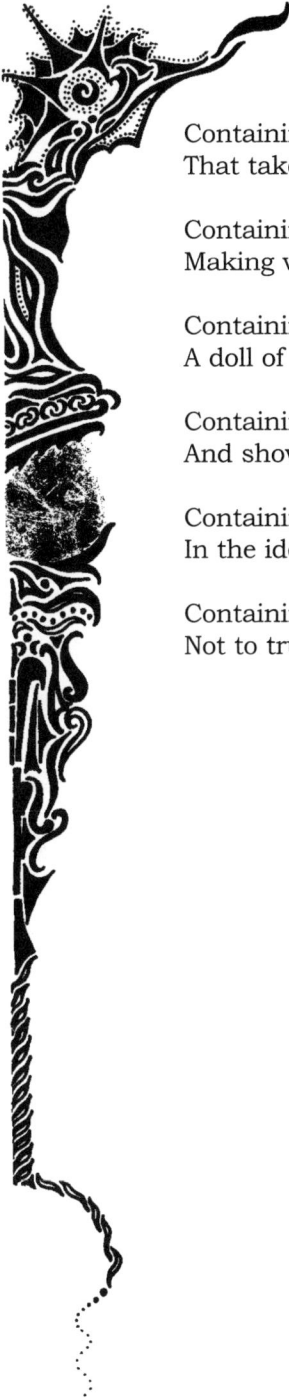

Containing random appearances of art
That take me when I can't do anything about it

Containing serenades of a saxophone player
Making velvet music on the mountain

Containing a homeless man selling to me
A doll of wires twisting in its dancing

Containing photographers of ice formations
And showroom dummies laughing hysterically

Containing Don Quixotes who see possibilities
In the ideas that make a person crazy

Containing fingers writing a warning
Not to trust your narrator

Part II

Journey into the Labyrinth

Fury Without Warning

We sit on a loaned sofa
Watching a television we hate to depend on
     Eating spaghetti that has stretched
Over days in a studio apartment
     We can barely afford
But from which we see the deer
     Mistaking us for innocence.

     Something unsettles you.
What, I don't remember.
     Maybe it was the guy I spoke to yesterday
Or how I should wash the dishes on my own time
     Or how I should wear something
That doesn't horribly clash or how I should demand
     From my new boss the popular schedule
Or the way I tore out the rent check
     Or things I shouldn't tell my mother.

     I alternate between a passive desire
To make it work and a bursting anger
     That spurs me into action
Yet the result is all the same.
     You smoosh food into my face.

     I would rather bury myself
Inside the hole in my heart
     So that the darkness protects me
From life, if this is life.
     I should not walk away or even turn away
Because then you are rejected
     But reject you is what I do.
And so you chase me around the room, crash into walls
     With one gripped fist barely holding on.
You tell me to calm down
     While I beg to be let go of
So that I might find a place in some nonexistent corner
     Or the porcelain bathroom sink
And bang my head to it, hoping it will let me in.
     Eventually you succeed in pinning me down.
My knees kick violently against your back
     And I thrash around not even human anymore.
You stifle me by hitting one palm then the other
     Across my swollen head for what seems hours

Until I lie limp in your grasp.
　　　There is nothing left to do
Yet from somewhere, I scream out in retaliation
　　　And you have to cover my mouth with both hands
And pinch my nose so I cannot breathe.
　　　You gather us up because you know
The cops are coming. You straighten the apartment,
　　　Turn stained pillows upside down,
Shove me into the bathroom to clean off food,
　　　Change clothes, cover black eyes and bloody lips.

　　　You know just what to do
As if you have faced them before.
　　　"No, officers, I attacked him."
They take you regardless
　　　And you ask me why
It's always the men they blame.
　　　I follow with borrowed bail and a neighbor
Who pretends to believe my embarrassing lies
　　　And looks at me like the white trash I am.
I draw blood to cleanse myself,
　　　To punish and control my own pain for once.

　　　I can still sleep through anything
But you are up wide-eyed and disturbed
　　　Contemplating the best course of action.
"It's time to go to Boston" you decide
　　　Where we will find a new life,
Friends, work, and school. Three days later
　　　Mother says good-bye, takes photos,
Looks confused, does not know what to expect
　　　And I call Father from the train station.
We have our bikes and my $4,000 college money
　　　That I earned working minimum wage before I met you.
It was my duty, as your wife, to make sacrifices for you.
　　　We always backed each other up against the world.
We were still learning and moving forward.
　　　No take-backs, we always said.

Paralysis

In domestic paralysis,
We fumble over each other.
Night's coolness hovers
In the stillness of it all.
In the invisibleness of it all,
We are blotched white across the sky.
Not white as in skin.
White as in colorless.
We have holes for eyes.
Our feet are kicked high.
The pain, our liquid,
Drips from the sky and smears.

Train Station

The hustling bustling train station
Was a foreign world to me,
Where everyone else had it together,
Where I learned to read *Elle* on magazine racks
To pretend I, too, was beautiful.

We rebuilt our bicycles from boxes.
We worked as a team as I deciphered his next moves.
We rode out of the station and rode into
Our apartment five days later
With all our belongings on us.

We were all foreigners in some way
At the youth hostel
While we hid our valuables from one another.
Yet we could still celebrate America together
Under blazing fireworks at Boston Harbor.

We attended Trinity Church and awed at the chorus.
I wondered if, like them, I could ever voice my voice.
The priest shook my hand as he greeted us at the door
And asked me if I was going camping.
I laughed with a smile but these rags were all I had.

For dinner, we shared a mango
On Newbury Street catwalk sidewalk.
Months later, we dressed in our best
For the elevator ride to the 50th floor of the Prudential Tower
Just to view the city sky through wealthy windows.

It took time learning to watch for passing trains.
On occasion, I got stuck on the tracks, oblivious
Like a deer blinded by headlights
Who doesn't know which way to turn
And thinks the blinding light may mean heaven.

MBTA to the Office

The Green Line.
The Orange Line.
The Red Line.
The Blue Line.

The Massachusetts Bay
Transportation Authority subway
Compresses us
From each direction.

We are inside a machine,
Inside a tunnel, breathing stale hot air.
It envelops scurrying workers
In a scurrying city.

Some of us commute for hours
Each day with the Boston Globe
In one hand and coffee
In the other.

The financial pages
Are amusement. Some of us are logical,
Bathing in numbers like gamblers
Who know there is always a chance.

Subway terminals smell of urine.
An old woman huddles on the concrete ground
With a trash bag for a home.
She waits for no train.

The screeching, shaking, swaying train
Announces arrival. A performer and his guitar
Request spare change. They are
More nomadic every day.

We consume the trains.
We are pushed aside for them by frantic hands,
By blank eyes that fear being left behind.
Survival is such a broad term.

The Day

Someone
Emerges from a wall
Makes coffee for two
Waves hello to a neighbor
Enters the Metro
Walks past a construction site
Waits at a street signal
Glimpses at a sculpture
Sits facing a machine
Rests on a park bench
Drinks a cola
Sits facing a computer
Glimpses at store window apparel
Waits at a street signal
Walks past a construction site
Exits the Metro
Waves hello to a neighbor
Gathers cans at a grocery mart
Dissolves into a wall
Someone
Gone, the day

Template

I speak from a template—
Into a receiver and out again.
Mechanical
Like rapid transit
From which we may scan
The images of our influence.
Rest then scan.
The images sift
Through my translucent head.
My head just sits there.
My head is an object
Reiterating the reiterated.
Anonymous.
A reflection of a template.
I wait for the operator.
We do not battle.
We do not have consciousness.
We digest each movement
Only to spit it out again.
Listen, archive, delete
Only to maintain the same template
Stainless as from the start.
I am sensory deprived
Like having my face
Bandaged in white plaster of paris
Conscious of nothing
Except my hand on a table
For balance
Like a child who cannot walk alone,
Like a model defining self-value
Based on what others think
Of a mold of a face on display.

GBS Factory

They sell in Japan, France, New York,
Los Angeles, San Francisco, and Boston.
The warehouse in Chinatown
Works with intention
To bring us the latest in fashion.
I can almost hear them swearing
In their hierarchy of glamour
As sewing machines
Pull garments through
And competitive designers push
For something you haven't seen before
But know you need.

I slip past the line of people
Waiting against the building with party invitations
Because I'm with the photographer
Then climb the wide wooden
Staircase to the third floor.
Once inside, there are dim lights, hypnotic music,
Rows of chairs, and plenty of wine.
I find the beauty queens
Smoking in the fire escape
Pretending they can't hear
More than my initial
Hello and embrace.

Crowds of beautiful guests
Competing for a glance their way
Fill the rooms and wear favorite clothing
Spoiled by what is found tonight.
I stroll up then down the runway
To let the photographer practice focusing
And they think I'm part of it all.
My conversations are short, trivial,
Usually about the wine or the factory
Or people we know in common
Or the last time I saw you at the Spring show
And how we both lose phone numbers.

A model walks in with a Japanese mask
Then faces us all to offer her dance.
One by one, they turn, reveal the fit
And kneel in appreciation
For our adoration.
We hold our breath for each new garment
And wish the model would stay a bit longer.
The zippers, the new line of boots, watches,
Inverted suits and inside-out shirts and winter skirts.
It's already Halloween and it's a celebration
Better than Newbury Street.

Generals of the Civil War

After bouncing over gutters and manholes,
I pedal my bicycle through public gardens.
 My skirt waves behind me.
  It flaps through Boylston Street
 And past statues of Yankee generals
Of the American Civil War who fought
 For freedom. They wink at me
  With sculpted eyes.

 Various men wake on park benches.
The black night was their blanket
 Covering every illness from the world
  For a few silent hours.
 I whiz past ringing, ringing my bell
Watching them yawn with unshaven faces
 And stretch in yesterday's clothing
  Before they decide on the day of Soup
 Kitchens and buddies with business to tend to.
All I do is find an old brick warehouse
 To lean against and later,
  A quiet office corner to hide out in
 To write on scraps of paper
About the ringing, ringing and then the silence
 Before someone finds me again
  As the being that I am.

 Morning greets us all
With her cool frosty breath, even the men
 On city park benches I ride past
  Who have freedom enough just to be.

The Beer Race

Just like any working class neighborhood
There were houses, lawns, and fences. BBQ parties
Thrived here and on almost any afternoon
One could smell hickory smoke trailing
Through air, creating an instantaneous hunger
In the mouths and stomachs of passersby.
It was frequently like 4th of July get-togethers
Unfolding during daylight hours.

Properties next to one another
Commonly exhibited colorful plastic lawn chairs.
One made a bet sitting on those chairs at times,
Depending on how many plastic loops
Were left attached to the metal frame.
"Steady now" one pleaded. "Be strong for me
Just once more and I promise
Not to wiggle too much."
Occasionally, though, a chair got stressed
One too many times and collapsed in exhaustion.
The result was that someone's ass
Thumped to the ground.
One might say that moment
Was the lawn chair's last triumph.
Once the beaming pride
Of a strong new plastic chair
Began dwindling over time, bodies grew heavier.
Eventually they were just unbearable.
The chair's final moment of glory and revenge
Was that collapsing
Thump into death whereupon the sitter
Then beamed red and surrounding peers
Roared with laughter
And clapped like thunder.

At the moment I passed by,
There were relaxed, non-committed interactions
Between BBQers. One guy
Sat watching me and my dog
Walk through the alley.
He tossed a softball in his hand by rolling it
Off his fingers and he never took his eyes off us.
So I simply acted like I didn't have a care.
I walked with a dip and pulled my hat

Further around my face while looking around
At the goings-on of yards and peoples.
He continued watching us
With an open laugh and a demeanor
That said "Hey, Vern. It's me, Earnest."
Then he looked at us with just one big eye
Like someone staring back at us
Sideways through the peephole of our own door.
A creepy little guy, if you ask me.
With softball tossing and turning in air
He challenged
"I bet my dog can outrace your dog
To find beer at the end of the alley and drink it down."
Now from my experience,
It seems best not to back away from bets
And challenges by backyard BBQers,
If one knows what I mean.
Either I could decline with a grin,
Walk away and pretend not to hear
Their chicken balking ridicule
Or I could perhaps one day join in their BBQ
Rendezvous, backyard talk, and card games
Yet I doubted if I would ever
Get to toss that softball.
Besides, most dogs probably like beer
And what better of a go-getter was there
Than my Golden Lab, Snicker Doodle?

We unleashed our dogs.
With tongues dripping, they were rarin' to go.
We had a chance of winning.
That dog didn't look so smart
But there they went.
Snicker Doodle hightailed
After this other guy's bulldog
As if it was the guide.

"Go get it, Banshee! You know how to do it!"
Banshee reached the alley's end
Defined by discarded tires and other car parts.
Like a rabid dog, she sniffed violently
Inside the black rubber tires
Until she crushed her teeth into an extra tall Coors.
Foam whizzed into her nostrils.
She gulped and growled
For Snicker Doodle to back off

Of what was rightfully hers.
        Earnest went off on a deep gutted laughter
                As if he knew the punch line to a favorite joke
        His buddy told and would ask his buddy to tell
To everyone who might not have heard it.
        Then like a young magician dying of secrecy
                He told his tricks.

"You see, Banshee don't ever listen to me
Unless she knows she's gettin' a cold beer. See.
        Watch. Banshee . . ." Whistle. Whistle.
                "Roll over . . . Beg . . . Shake . . . Play dead . . .
        See. Nothin'. Nothin' at all. She just looks at ya.
It took me a long time to realize she wasn't deaf.
        She just knows what she wants
                And she knows when I don't got it."
        We wandered back to the BBQing lawn chair group.
He grabbed another beer from the ice chest,
        Held it over Banshee and said "Play dead."
                Banshee ran around in circles and I thought
        She had mistaken the command for "Chase tail."
Then she fell motionless to the ground
        With face and body completely relaxed.
                It was kind of eerie.
        Then she leapt straight out of napping position
And snatched beer out of hand. I was flabbergasted.
        I truly was and I clapped
                Like it was the end of the Super Bowl.

"See" he said with a tilt of the head.
"You just gotta know how to treat your friend right,
        Give 'em what they want."
                With that, Earnest and Banshee
        Indulged in another round of BBQ.
Snicker Doodle looked up at me like I was hiding
        A beer in my jacket and wasn't gonna give it up.
                So on the way home, we stopped
        At the QuickiMart for a 6-pack
Then trailed off to our own backyard.
        Maybe we could both learn
                A few new tricks, I thought.

The Race

"So how are you doing in the race so far?"
Grandfather asked.

"What race?"
I inquired.

"Ha! Ha! Ha! The human race."
Grandfather answered.

Perhaps I missed out on that one.
Most of the time, I am racing my selves
And I hope to win, too
Although the others can be quite sneaky.

The Door

After the swimming hole
We stopped at the country market.
I questioned "Ma'am,
May I use the restroom?"
The Ma'am answered
"Yes. Go through those double doors
And then the brown door
And then the other door."
I stepped through the double doors.
There were three brown doors in the room.
To each I stepped through I found another door
And there was always someone to greet me.
"Sir, which way do I go?"
The Sir answered "Go through that brown door
And then the other door."
Through the brown door
There were two other doors in the room.
One was posted "Restroom."
I stepped through.
After my duties I stepped back
Out of the double doors.
I did not get trapped by their maze.
I continued driving down the road
After finding my way.

Philosophy Class

Socrates, Plato, Aristotle.
SPA
The professor writes
As he breaks chalk frantically on diagrams,
Dances with energy,
Points at texts,
And asks why we have not
Soaked them in our own ink.
He buzzes through rows of seating
Like the mosca after mosca
He has learned from.
I spin and grow dizzy as I swat in circles.
I am bitter from reading and testing
On what I cannot comprehend
And so I offer not a word, not ever.
He might discover my obliviousness.
All I do is laugh on the other side of the door
While questioning
If the door is really there and why.
I laugh at the phantoms fabricating my world
And I sit, amused
At others' inability to get on with life
Since life and the classroom
Must be two separate worlds unaffecting each other.
Once the testing is over and I am relieved
To study more applicable subjects,
I hurl books to the wall.
I throw them furiously and stomp with soles,
With muddy boots that rip and shred
Ridiculous pages. Philosophy
Destroys everything I have to rely upon.
I have to erase its mark
Before it sinks in
And crushes my pretty life.

Hands

Dough on flour is molded into the nude
Before it is toiled with on the ground floor of survival
And told to be covered out of moral concern.
I am placed on a predetermined path
On which my dreams are interpreted.
Yet instead, I stray into the forest
With Young Goodman Brown.
I walked the halls of education
And tried the pride ring on my wedding finger.
Tight fit. I could not get it off.
I laughed. Now my hand was to be cut off
For coloring outside the lines.
There was a whirlwind of some sort
Which caused my legs and limp body
To follow some unknown path.
Do I perceive beyond
Into the various realities
Of the kaleidoscope of life and break new trail?
Or am I lucky enough to see
Only between the borders
And out of mental sanity remain in that state?
In a struggle, I am destined to lose once hearing the voice
Of Siren, a singing temptress.
It was merely a game.

The Unseen Gate

Shivering wings flutter over her tracks
Searching like a hawk for the unseen gate.
Azure and coral in sky seem to mate
Before the storm rages and contracts.

A path of depression so desperate, so patched
Intends to fail freedom and pain is bait.
She descends, does not recognize the rate
And gates of self-realization again are latched.

Independence remains an easy fantasy.
She desires to secure her mind with faith
But hope of liberty is absent, only a blind path
Where time clenches her sanity. "I want to see!

Open the gate!" she demands of any face near
And a hawk falls to the soil, but cannot hear.

Those Eyes

Who you are or what you are
Is not known to me.
You twinkle
Then you are obscene
And unpredictable.
You move through this house
Knowing it is yours
Yet the offer terrifies you.
It is the offer of the better.
The offer is too much,
Not real, you say.
You expect yourself to fail.

I gaze upward
Wishing you, too, could see stars.
You want to be
Outside yourself
But do not know
Where you would go.
Hands reach out of walls
Asking you to stay.
You are not ready to go
But you go and still
You do not see the stars.
You do not smell fresh air.

Your range of motion is limited.
Part of you remains atrophied.
Sometimes eyes
Are in the skin
But you were told
Not to trust those eyes,
Not to believe what you see
But you should believe.
You should demand to know
Truth inside of you,
Not as some
Far away thing.

Hang In There

Days of distress and days of want—
One by one they choose their paths.
Don't say to me your words of regret
That cure and polish like a cut.
In the end I will be free
Of burdens that choke the spirit.
Behind those walls so thick,
We all are children who trusted once
And now we hide deep in our hearts
Surviving in a world that silences us.
Still we fight for those who see,
For those who penetrate the inner being
And keep this promise that was meant
To be kept by all who want,
By all who feel distress.

My Marionette

She stood facing
The spotted mirror
Applying and wiping,
Wanting approval of
Already exquisite features.
I knew the various tears of anxiety
Could never rust her,
Never overbear her
For she was stronger than that.
She often detested me
And the choices I would make for her.
She was under my control
Savoring the every smile I offered her.
Grey madness, absurdity was what she believed in,
Was what the man in me
Would always override
For just her annoyance,
Her klutzy, irrevocable ways
Helped me comprehend her need for me,
And I loved her, solemnly.

Years Ago
(The Only Insurance a Woman Had Was Her Husband)

Entwined in devotion is the chic couple
As they attend a garden of vine and health
While mingling and adding illusion
To their dynamics.

Yet that is merely the public appearance
Of hostile rather than sound relations.
Perhaps the sacrifice is much too deep
And desire builds in territory elsewhere.

She holds pose abidingly
Curious of the locked disposition and its finality.
Her mask finds identity within his life,
Claiming it as her chosen own.

This must be her duty so she does not complain
Of the blotched reality encompassing her
But instead, continues to taste his sultry breath.
She is both his pleasure and his anger.

Smoky is the enclosed air
For their life smells of a cigar—stale.
Still, she simply waits for cues in the so-called
Magnificent lights of her dreams.

Relaxation can deliver peace to mind
Briefly until he awakens by the night train.
Fighting truth, he continues
In a fit of jealousy.

Trivial subjects toy with his emotions
For his heart is constructed of insecurities and swears
He must control her indecency. She accepts blame
And is reminded of her dependence on him.

Bruises and bandages bind her body
Yet it is he who claims of being
Sifted through broken glass.
Sight blurs more each passing day.

Hideous colors solidify their existence.
She cannot forget the tombstones of competition
For her advancement in a field of his
May prove more of a disturbance.

Bitter sweat drips off his chin.
The shouting is now over.
Her hands wrap around evidence of disorder
To discard the ripped garments.

They can never eliminate the gap
Between reality and appearance.
He does not accept the imperfections before him.
She stands and walks to the door.

Will she sway one day to ask for help
In learning the truth she hardly knows exists?
Or will she collapse into an irreversible state
Where her blind numb senses give in to anything?

A limp neck bends toward home
Through staircases and stone bridges
Adjacent to the city, then repels the thought.
Shadows of disbelief dart across the terrain.

With a friend, she slips the secret into conversation
And awakens choices that now entice her
In contrast to the rigid suffocation
That she once expected as a part of companionship.

A Queen. A Palace. A Prisoner.

There were no
      temptations to reject, no noticeable lack
        of pleasure.
      Analyzing literature
   was a method of escape, not
a connection to myself.
  I didn't feel a thing, not
     even the repulsive
       awkward touches
     that never quite fit, not
   even the violent fighting words
in the crowded subway directed
   at some lonely kid who stood
      on the steps mumbling, not
        even the absence of friendship
    since your eyes always
   signaled for me to follow
you through the room while monitoring
  like an officer of love, patrolling
      my indecent notice of others
       and my crippled
    stunted phrases. I
  was your glamorous make-up
artist although the models must
  have been laughing. I
     was your symbol of liberality
      while you bragged
    of my feministic role
  as long as I
never made us an example. I
  was your transfixed keyhole
    but you thought you could get
      through the stone door. I
   was your financial security
  every time you lashed out
against culture's definition of prosperity. So I
   bought you camera equipment,
    crowning your self image
      with lenses lighting props
    while we bounced checks
  at the grocery store but I
left you with scars for us both. Now
  I admire anonymity while eating

to fulfill a hunger for love. Now
I consume
lots of bitter beer and cigarettes.
I buy back books and music
from when I didn't care.
I am surrounded by friends.
I am entranced by them all—
everyone you wouldn't like
and I laugh in hysteria
as the wandering womb enters my head
and takes control further out of your hands.
I sit for hours flexing fingers
staring at white walls
just because I can.

Rose's Collage

Perhaps she wanted dreams to fly
When she met this person.
Perhaps she only wanted to fly
Away from this person
But felt she had no choice.
She didn't have physical wings
And didn't believe strongly enough
In metaphors so day by day life
Was restricted and excavated
By this other person.
He controlled all her money, spent it all.
He told her who her friends were,
Acted wary of them all out of insecurity,
Called her names and gave her bruises
But her bones were much too strong
For him to break.

She was a tattered woman
With a numb face who wore war paint
Dawn through dusk
And sometimes into night.
At times she resembled a mannequin
Used for this or that purpose
But not feelingless and not heartless.
The mannequin is someone
Else's trophy to display.
At times she also resembled a marionette
With strings operated by a puppeteer.
She danced around and sang
A little song because her job
Was to impress and thus,
She made the puppeteer proud
Of his dolly, for a moment.

Secretly in the back dressing room
When changing between costumes,
She joined with other mannequins
And marionettes
To form an alliance
To escape from the love-hate dance.
Today breaks up yesterday's bondage,
Melts it with her steamy breath.

Women held hands in a circle,
Danced, cried, and told each other stories
    Until they developed clever plans
        To sneak away one by one.
    Some felt so tainted, dirty, and deceptive
For turning away from the puppeteer
    But they also began to feel fabulous
        And time can do so much.

    Now she sees others without shoes
During midnight escape.
    Another escape artist finds slippers
        To provide cushion for feet,
    Eats soup from a can,
Makes milk from a box,
    And slips into a bed waiting for her.
        Some have no interest
    In support groups or counseling.
A mattress, a meal, and an ear that will listen
    Are enough for now.
        All other concerns are pushed aside
    Into the forgotten library
Of the long-term memory
    Where they will, no doubt
        Show up until they are dealt with.

    Here, a woman is a fugitive
From her own home built
    With her four-chambered heart,
        With blood and with bruises
    Yet she meets new people where she goes,
Whether she likes them or not.
    There is crying, tension,
        Silence, sharing, and moving.
    "Who are these people?" she asks.
They got here by calling a phone number
    Someone handed to them in secret.
        There was no name attached
    To the seven-digit number
Which sometimes is a door from here to there
    Amongst the endless doors
        Before and after this one.

    Here she is after telling an ear
A deep dark secret on the telephone.
    She could no longer deny a truth

Revealing itself behind
Purple silk curtains
Because she did not one day want
The curtains to reveal a murder mystery.
A voice on the other end of the phone
Guaranteed nothing but a matress,
A bite to eat, a toothbrush,
And more phone numbers.
Others here may or may not
Be friends yet they eat together,
Cry together, and perhaps might not
See each other again until
They are stars in the sky.

She wants to be anonymous.
Her phone number is unpublished.
Her social security number is changed.
She hopes her abuser
Cannot find her now.
She must find therapy for her damaged soul,
Health-care for her broken-down body,
And clothes to replace
The ones ripped off her.
Although detoxing from an abuser may be lonely,
Depressing and terrifying, now she may go
Where she pleases and talk
With whom she pleases.
She is poor and free, free from expecting
Idealism where it cannot be found.
She is victorious.

Rose's healing process includes a collage.
This was a support group project
To be completed in a two-hour period
But she cannot put it away
Unless she rests also.
At night, the collage sleeps with the sewing supplies.
Newspaper and magazine clippings
Dance with her soul day into night.
To her, this is music.
She is a drum with ribbons tied into her hair.
She is a colorful collage
Photocopied into black and white.
She is framed in red for this is her blood life.
She is black and white and bordered by red.
She is the news that never
Entered the newspaper.

Volcano

In the sea and on land
Earth's surface holds tight until
Fires burst from its center.
Molten lava flows.
Magma thrusts into sky.
Earth is like a silly child trying
Her darnedest not to laugh,
Not to give away
The secrets of life
Until finally she bursts
At the seams giggling like
A natural disaster.

Phantom

There is a key
With which the phantom runs
On a jagged route.
I follow, chasing
This phantom as though
My essence is about to escape.
Time seems to close in yet
It keeps on ticking.

I stand
And accuse others
Of the behaviors I fear in myself,
Working to control
What I find a threat.
"Bring that phantom back here!
It ought to face a trial
For the truth it grasps!"
My external upper deck
Verbalizes this insanity.
My internal lower deck
Cowers and frets
With unrecognized jealousy
And is veiled by anger
And an attempt to control.
This merging of decks
Displays itself
In strange ways
Such as fear of the phantom self
Running to hide the key
From the dictator.
Seeking myself in the ocean,
I peer over the railing of the ship
Into a mirror of coded language.

If logic is in the brain
And passion is in the heart
How can I think logically
About passion?

Captain Ahab knew
That the mysterious white whale
He sought was the mystery
Inside himself
Making him insane.
Now I, too, spend frequent hours
Studying navigational literature
And rewriting it.

Joy Division

You know she lost control
With that fetish for yard sales,
Junk yards and hardware stores.
Trying to make sense of scraps,
She straps her collections
To the bicycle with a bungee cord
While never accomplishing
The task she left the house to do.
Then she takes you by the hand,
Gives away the secrets of her past,
And expresses herself in various ways
With the beats, the dim smiles,
The glasses she can see through.
Her love tore her apart.
So she speaks of herself
In 3rd person. Yet she refuses
To become digital, to become
A calculable statistic, a number with no face.
And she knows that home
Is wherever she makes a home.

Charlotte's Wallpaper

Charlotte Perkins Gilman walks along.
Digits extend from hands.
One foot follows the other.
When she wears a night slip
Or an expensive black gown
Or artist clothing covered in paint
With fresh daisies in her pocket
Is she the same woman?

It's all about the card deck.
Queen of Diamonds or Queen of Hearts?
No one can tell until the card flips over
Showing its frontal design.

She shared the era she was born into
With therapists who believed a woman
Was cured of her madness through total rest
And therefore placed women
Into hermetic isolation
Until behaviors resembled
That of the perceived acceptable norm.
Charlotte was not allowed
To do a thing so that
She might get better and do away with silly fancies.
She even had to be secretive about writing
Since that may have been
What made her sick.
Yet for many women, this lack of activity
Was the very thing causing
So much disquiet.

Charlotte studied the yellow wallpaper
In her room that was formerly a nursery.
She described the wallpaper as repellent,
Unclean and strangely faded from the sun
Not like the yellows in the garden
That had tansies and evening primroses.
Nocturnally and slowly,
Charlotte discovered a woman
Moving behind the wallpaper and shaking it.
Charlotte started creeping by night,
Wearing out the wallpaper,
Getting yellow on her clothing

And carrying with her a funny smell.
Eventually she crept by day as well
On that long imagined road out of doors
And wrote about herself in 3rd person.
She stared into yellow wallpaper at night.
Sometimes wallpaper is the only true sign of life
With patterns and sub-patterns,
Tours and detours
And a figure that lurks beneath.
There has to be a garden plastered on the wall
When the organic ones
Can no longer be reached.
Wallpaper remains intact
As the same image rising
Every morning with the sun
Unless it gets torn down
By venting, raging palms and digits
Or worn off by the pacing, pacing
Hopeful notion that one may slip
Out of this and into that.

Metamorphosed
Figures within figures
Became the ultimate reality
For a woman sentenced
To several months of rest therapy.
Charlotte knew there was more
Than just a frontal design of herself,
Of this emerging wallpaper
So she tore it down to avoid
Being put back behind it
Day after night like a prisoner.
Her husband fainted at the sight
Of this creeping about.
As a woman struggling
To move forward into tomorrow
And break free from patterns,
She crept right over the top of him
Then continued her journey
On hands and knees
Rubbing up against the walls
That bound her and that was where
She made her mark.
She made small movements
Which eventually grooved into walls.

Now, a path is a bit more unraveled
For the rest of women
Who don't want to be put
Back into the wallpaper.

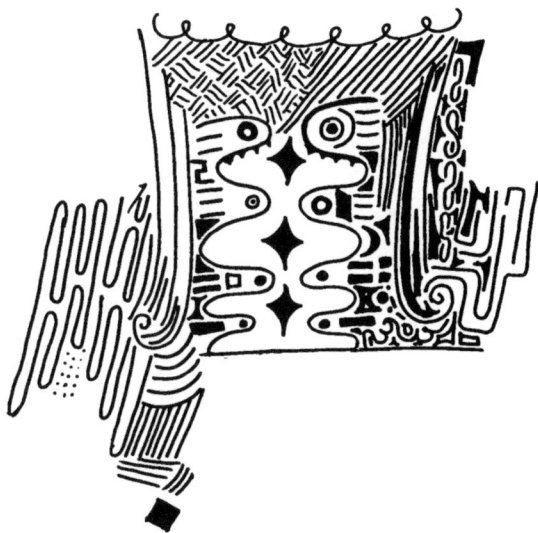

Part III

Echo of the Spiral

On Sera's Portrait

I saw a woman's face today
Garmented by her movements within.
  She seemed to thrive on a plane
    Parallel to her ideologies
  Without separating head from heart.
Who could do that but a woman
  Who conquers her boundaries?
    She knows the intangible
  Ambiguity of suffering
As well as the infinite charms of life
  That rediscover themselves
    Through mythology
  And reach into all points at once
To hug the indispensable Universe.
  Would not Orpheus
    Descend into Hades again
  For Eurydice even knowing
His transcending music
    Was part of a fated game to the gods?
    Now we replay
  Mythology and shape it
Through empowerment when fate
  Holds the hands
    Of knowledge and decision.
  You see, that is her secret
Although she shares it
  With a thousand others
    Who practice
  This kind of healing.
She begins by restitching
  The bruised and calloused body
    Back to the insensible mind
  And by pulling out the thorns.
This woman has two decipherable mouths
  Formed out of the flesh which speak
    Fluidly in simultaneous tongues.
  One mouth transforms intellect
And reason into notes that others may follow
  While the opposite mouth
    Moves in rhythms,
  Spiritually embracing and marking
All dimensions. Many people wonder
  How they lie in connection

With each other.
All wonder, in fact, except those
Who also walk in waves
In order to select among the roses
And avoid being cut
By the same thorns
Again and again. Regardless,
All have been cut
Or will be cut.
So you see, this woman descends
Into Hades for her own Eurydice.
Scarlet for her roses.
Scarlet for her blood.

Cherries

Red is my blood
That does not settle.
    Perhaps it began
        With the cherries we ate.
    Or perhaps it began
Long before that. I picked
    Deep red cherries one day
        While sitting on shoulders
    Of a friend. I picked
The ripest ones while looking
    Over the fence at
        The neighbor's lawn party.
    From fingers to mouths to bellies
We ate cherries from the tree
    Then continued training
        Our martial arts on the grass.
    We ate cherries from the tree
Like the ones Mother and I
    Picked on the farm.
        We ate cherry tomatoes
    On kabobs for picnic
And cherry tomatoes in salad
    Exploding in mouths.
        Cherries are the color
    Of my shirt even before
I read my horoscope telling me to yell
    "My Passion is my Fashion!"
        Even the fabric
    I wrap my painting in
Is red like the fire engines I pass
    Before driving over Mt. Hood Pass.
        The sun sets in the West
    With reds and oranges against the range.
Thundering sky complements
    With hues of blues and grays
        Like my polyester skirt
    To my cherry shirt.
Cherry is the maple leaf
    On the Canadian flag.
        Cherry is my figure in Candyland.
    Cherry is your trim dress
Dancing behind me
    As your long hair blows around me
        And I curl back in layers.

Trumpet Player

It's the lady in the vintage shop I go to see
Not the velvet dresses and see-through shoes.
    I go to see her cherry lipstick
        Move with articulate hands.
    She speaks of our inherent nature
Advancing always toward some sense of being,
    Even if a choice of retreating
        Signifies a motion elsewhere.
    She asks if speaking of pleasure
Brings up different emotions
    In various languages, as if language
        Is a dimension of its own,
    As if language is a beauty of its own.
She asks if music is heard
    Distinctly new to each ear
        As notes get swept away
By the brush of a moment,
Invisibly escaping into infinity
    Yet always remaining in existence.
        I wish I could write
    Like the trumpet player
Whose jazzy composition
    Fluctuates as he breathes.
        He seems conscious of all
    As he takes in and pushes out.
He is ignited by eager eyes
    And clapping hands.
        His head beats
    And shakes to the rhythm.
He travels with the beat
    Of the drummer
        And the saxophone player.

The Bathroom

It's a fiasco.
All is . . . all is complex.
Not even the paper I write on
Is straightforward and absolute.
Its pre-birth blankness tells me novels.
The mingling voices of friends
Are like portraits telling stories.
The characters come
With digestive tones and reflexes.
They feed off one another
And compile energy variously.
Cool black night
Seeps through windows
At my side and teases my skin.
Smokey scented air
Teases my mind.
I bounce from smiles to oiled canvases
To fashion attire to sporadic segments
Of wandering conversations.
I cannot follow any of them
Because I hear all at once.
I bounce all the way to the bathroom
Where segments rejoin in a paradox.
Below me to the left as I twist
Stands a five inch silver mirror on a tripod
Whose image turns as I turn and does not lie.
Before me is a display of Catholic icons.
Rosaries dangle from the necks
Of Mother Mary and Saint Christopher.
Then I turn to face a gigantic monstrous hand
Leaping out of the corner.
It hovers over
The porcelain bathtub
Like a swampy figure that will not drown.
I ask myself why it is monstrous.
Its appearance is strange to me
And possibly represents the fears
Of my own threatened imagination.
I am culturally trained to recognize it
As dehumanizing and vengeful
Because it is ugly to my senses
Yet it wears the most glamorous rings.

Again, my ability to judge value
Is questioned.
The whole peculiar room
Questions value.
Is this a paradox
Or is it complementary?

Out of the Past

We pace our steps to railroad ties
With one foot in front of another.
　　　Occasionally a steam engine
　　　　　Rolls along and puffs its smoke
　　　Trailing the half-lit sky,
Shifting like liquid.
　　　The train rumbles by pulling cargo
　　　　　From one destination to another.
　　　It transports through urban stations
With escalators and marble floors and great clocks.
　　　It transports through mountains,
　　　　　Beside rivers and
　　　Paved roads of vehicles
With rubbernecks viewing
　　　A relic out of the past.
　　　　　It passes over the burial of time
　　　Filled with tools and bones
And tales of other ages.
　　　The train signals its transporting
　　　　　With a whistle
　　　That urges children
To lay pennies on tracks
　　　And farmers to check
　　　　　Their cows and fences.

We pace our steps to railroad ties
Until we curve toward the river.
　　　Mud on boots tells of the journey.
　　　　　The dock sways.
　　　City lights twinkle on the opposite shore.
A boat spelling NOEL in strings of bulbs glides by
　　　With cheering passengers.
　　　　　A handmade paper lamp drifts
　　　On this river of time.
It reads HAPPY NEW YEAR 2000.
　　　It was made in the old world
　　　　　To seek out the new.

Passage

Time is beyond
The falling of leaves
And ground foraging.
Time enters
Into a world
That yields to quiet.
Such a pale warmth
Solitude is.

Snow covers Earth
Layer upon layer
To allow rest
And rebirth
Into Spring.
These seasons, like light
And dark, complement
One another.

All the gates
Between various worlds of the soul
Are there if we have
Power to see them.
Some glimmer
And others are so faint.
Gates are the means
Of entrance and exit.

One gate stands
With spikes topped with snow.
Pillars alongside
This gate are roofed
With a dome of snow.
It stands open.
A set of tracks
Lead in and out.

Ivy spirals the pillars.
They sparkle white,
Are coated with frost,
Numbed
To the world a while.
Organic patterns of nature
Cling a little more
Each passing year.
I walk tall, pass in between
With hands open, welcoming
The lighted tree of my soul.
It is both
Pain and joy
To behold. It lights the dark
Like a wizard's staff
In winter's cold peace.

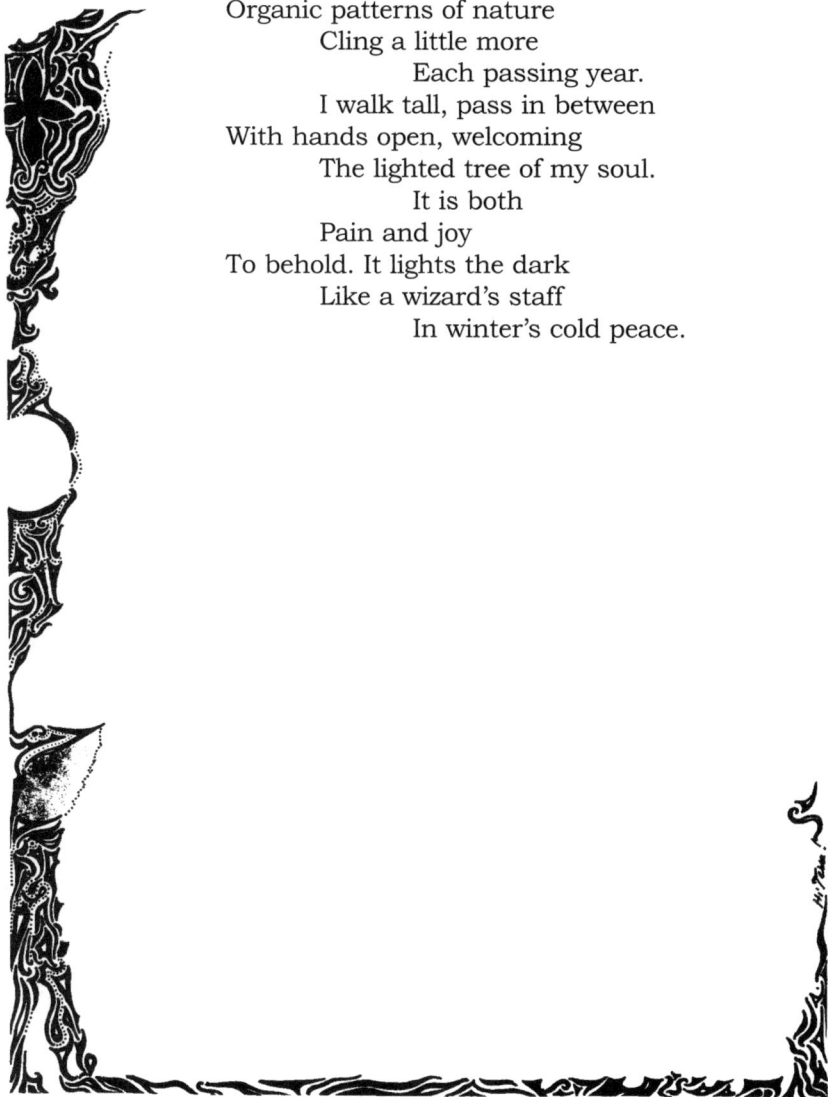

Stepping of the Soul

She sits in a candle-lit room
With an imagination of colors
To provide a spellbinding
Internal atmosphere.
Sometimes colors mingle, shifting
In stormy winds of subconsciousness
So that shades of grays
Loom
Over centuries of thoughts.
From one corridor of the maze
In her mind into another
She sees
What she has not seen
Before or perhaps she sees
Everything again,
For the future
Is the past manipulated
By the spinning wheels of chance.
She knows all is chance
While knowing
All is more than chance.
She steps forward into night into day.
Soil, dust, and ash
Feather
Around her steps making trail.
Who knows what lay buried
Beneath the stepping of her sole.
Who knows what lay buried
Beneath the stepping of her soul.
For the passing of time is a burden
For the passing of time is a blessing
And only history
Can accurately depict history.
The remainder is contorted memory
And centuries of ghosts.
What does exist
Are layers of fossils,
Tools and bones beneath the stepping.
What does exist
Is creation in process.
Here occurs
The glimpsing into eternity
While telling a single tale

Of the human experience.
She courses through the maze
In her mind so that she might become
A part of all she comes in contact with
So that when her bones
Lie down like ash,
Her ghost may remain
Like a warrior
In wandering wind.

The voice
Is a communication, a weapon, an art.
        Even the rooster sounds out
With its freedom to sing.
        One has to take care of
The voice.
        One must not forget it exists.
The voice
        Sings Christmas carols
To the other side
        Of an open door
Decorated with wreaths, holly,
        And angels watching over.
The voice
        Sings Handel's *Hallelujah.*
The voice
        Sings summer campfire songs.
The voice
        Told me at age 13
That it would write a book.
        It refused to pantomime.

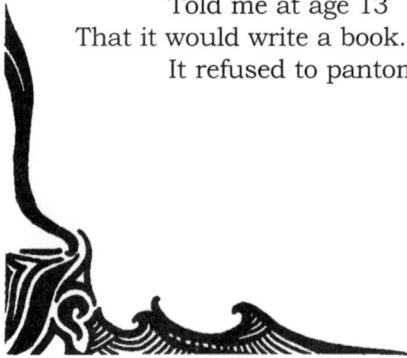

Tattoo Studio

Open studio on the second floor
Exhibits photos of the best work.
Corner windows
Hint at pounding rain.
I smell nothing except a sterile void—
White floors and white counters.
Everything is scrubbed down
Except drawing boards.
I lie with head on arm
Sweating from heat and excited tension.
Tricky's hypnosis distracts my mind.
Decorations on the arm, back, leg—
Celtic lines, Viking horses and
A woman's face I've never seen.
It's a declaration—
Inner undeniable blood.
The needle does not pretend sensitivity.
Endorphins seep through me
So I grant them domination.
I transform a bold emphatic craving—
My brand, my identity,
Woman who runs off
With the Viking horses.

Amusement Park

As a spectator of city sidewalk chaos
I am freely amused by your movements
Regardless of your consent.

Rhythms chant of your condition
Beating on the buckets and sinks
Of your make shift drum set.

Today I saw you with a patriotic plastic banner
Wrapped around your waist while you bent over
And used some cord to beat broken sidewalk glass.

You transport your twisted self this way or that,
Gliding with daily ritual or offset with distraction.
Time seems an issue regardless of purpose.

Some of you, perhaps all of you, are straying transients
Carrying on with your eclectic activity
Which so sweetly upsets your business.

Some Wear Books

People dress themselves variously.
Some dress in the latest fashion from runways
Of Paris, Milan, and New York.
Some wear business suits, ties,
And wing tip shoes.
Some wear evening gowns, stiletto heels, and handbags.
Some wear flaring pants and platform shoes.
Some wear the same outfit
For countless days until offered newer garments
From a church or social organization
Along with soup and bread.
Some wear cowboy boots and a hat
And some wear no more than that.
Some wear skintight leather and a long whip.
Some dress in drag.
Some dress in drag
Back to their birth gender.
Some wear tattoos, otherwise literally naked.
Some wear whatever is available.
Others want nothing that is available.
Some wear televisions and computers.
Some wear vacuum cleaners and laundry carts.
Some wear wine glasses and serving trays.
Some wear books and manuals
And for each one that is read
Five more are next in line on bookshelves
Extending out like extra arms.
People dress themselves variously.

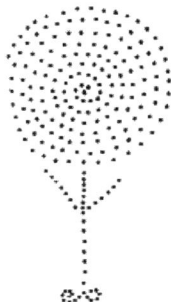

Box

Here is a box and one may guess what is inside.
Everyone will have a different idea about the contents.

People		Join
Together		On the
Foundation		Of Earth
With many		Colors
And build		the walls
With ideas and		knowledge
To protect		what is
Inside		the box.

Here is a box and one may guess what is inside.
Everyone will have a different idea about the contents.

Easter Tulips

On a rectangle box
I painted Easter Tulips stretching tall
In shades of pink.
When I put
The box near the wall
We could see Tulip shadows
Marking all the way
Past the ceiling.
Then hands took the box
Turning it in each direction
So that what I painted
Were so many pictures
Such as Earth with a crescent Moon
And a night train making its way
Through mountains
Of seasonal colors.

Framework

I was once dazzled
By bright city lights like 4th of July sparklers.
"Oohs" and "Aahs" floated inside the Pontiac
Along with a pine air freshener.
My family crossed bridges
Stretching toward the center of a 5-star buffet
Of opportunity and charm.
Even from a distance I explored
Towering skylights and created
Imaginative narratives about the array of possibilities.
There must be something for everyone
In such a place.

When people in this city go somewhere,
Some pause along the way at construction sites
Where buildings are built up during day.
From a sidewalk cliff
Some people are drawn to look
Through an interweaving metal fence.
A canyon of construction workers
Wear hardhats
And yellow-orange,
The color of a warning sign.
Pounding. Sawing. Hammering.
Look out below!

Construction echoes against
The framework of our culture.
There seems no hesitancy
In crafting the city,
Where options are many.
We dig deep into Earth,
Dig ourselves a giant hole and fill it
With an abstractly articulated manifesto.
Up rises a monument to the city.
Some people pause in promenading to and fro
To recognize another investment in the future.
Another skyscraper reaches farther

Toward heaven and the stars as if we hope for
Advanced communication.
A drizzle from above
Recognizes all it falls upon
Including the artwork
Of architects,
Construction workers,
And secretaries.
It is as if
We are in a rain dance.

From a crane hang lines of the imagination
Whereupon the subconscious speculates
As to what all this means.
It's a new opportunity
Not to be missed because perhaps
This will be one more hammered nail
Toward completion. I look through
The protective safety wire fence
Fragmenting vision. I look
Into construction in order to comprehend
The core of it all,
How it is built.

Radio Station

Everything rattles
From the fax machine printing
To the honking, the motors, the telephone.
"I'm taking a break"
I mumble halfway out the door
After leaving the phones to voice mail
And leaving the regular dependable view
To a few withering plants.

I walk with the street signals
While glancing into building
Exit ways and store windows.
Some folks scurry
With watches and bags.
Other folks play melodies
On guitars or flutes
Or sell flowers with smiles.
The melodies reach
All the way to the square—
A city block of bricks
With stairs for chairs.

Look! Over there!
A radio station brought
A blow-up animated whale.
It must be a friendly gray whale
Personified with smile
And cool sunglasses.
It stands erect on its tail
Like a begging dog.
Ties connect it to the ground
So it doesn't float away
Into another world.
The radio station brings action.
A blinking yellow signal
On top the van proves it to us,
Speaking—
Action! Action!

Another van
Backs up the tarped stage area.
It is painted as an orange and yellow
Checkerboard and displays the happiest
Faces you have ever seen in your life
Then displays the lettering
"The joke's on us!
Laugh your head off!"

From coast to coast
In cities during summers
Crowds gather to receive free bottles of juice.
One may even stock a backpack
By returning to barrel and representative
As though for the first time.
Next for the show,
Two basketball mascots wrestle
In blow-up padded suits.
The crowds gather and ask
"What is going on here?"
It's such a nice day
For free entertainment
That comes directly
To me and to you
And needs no extra effort.

Yet there are other duties to tend to
The guide knows.
She does not allow her students
To miss the train
Because of a mere distraction from reality.
Behind the square's wall of brick seating
Where one may observe
Without becoming involved,
An electric train called Max
Speaks out in digital voice
"The doors are now closing."
It continues on its route.

Piggies in the Bathtub

We sit on the side of the porcelain bathtub
To soak our feet in salt so that instead of being too tired
To go to the market, our piggies will giggle
All the way there and all the way home.

Do you see?
This is where I once had blisters layered on blisters.
Here on my ball of foot and arch
From running, running, running.

Do you see?
This is where I once had blisters on skin rubbed raw
Above the heel from speed walking in new shoes
Made for the Beautiful People.

Do you see?
These are the knots on outside edges of feet
From moving between standing, zealot, standing.
This marble breaks loose tension.

This is the marble
In bathtub in bathroom in house in neighborhood
In city in state in country in continent
In planet in galaxy in universe.

In a dream, I float in space
And listen to a narrator who mumbles how small we are,
Who points to a dot on a map and says
"You Are Here."

Yet piggies are happy with their bathtub soak.
They care not of significance.
The piggies balance the world
As they giggle on their way.

Feet

In a rustic barn
A Polled Hereford lies on straw,
    Finds shade for her thick bovine hide
        Then stands in a corral
    Muddy from an overflowing water trough
And I add to it by hosing her down,
    Down to a wire figure eight
        Wrapped around her ankle.

    At a gate, an Appaloosa works
The latch with her mouth just to stand
    On the other side. Then she limps
        So I take the hoof pick to her
    Until I find the frog, then clip and file,
Pull out the nail, soak her foot in Epsom salt,
    Shoot penicillin into her neck
        And see my reflection in her eyes.

    On a pipe trailer, a 10-year-old-girl
Dangles her carefree legs while bouncing over
    Rugged grooves of a Crooked River Ranch dirt road
        With views of Three Sisters,
    Mt. Bachelor, Mt. Jefferson, Broken Top
Until the wheel grabs at her foot, rotating
    But she is only sprained.
        Injury is minimal, heals quickly.

    In a studio apartment,
A bloodthirsty pit bull found its way into another's home
    And locked its jaws on a Persian cat's leg.
        The studio filled up with neighbors
    And the day filled up with hospitals.
Yet with only three legs and a tail,
    She still climbs a ladder to a loft
        And purrs into grateful ears at night.

Buffet Flats

Buildings on the side of Highway 97
Were painted cubist black and white,
Were painted like graffiti art.
That is, until the highway
Was widened for the growing driving population
Who wished the country would remain rural
For their children and grandchildren.
They hoped life would remain real.

Many folks wondered who would enter a building
Such as Buffet Flats with collages of concepts.
After pleading with curiosity,
Mother took me for a brief visit
With mannequins in costumes.
This event gave birth to a fascination
For junk antique shops and all the characters
That dance inside when we aren't looking.

A miniature TV set shows *The Wizard of Oz*
Inside a four-story dollhouse not for sale.
Even the geography professor wanders off
On Dorothy and her little red shoes
Walking the yellow brick road. He clicks
His own two heels three times together then comes back home
To realize there is no more Buffet Flats
On one side of the highway.

The folks moved across the street
And opened the Funny Farm
Like a city couple moving to the country.
Dorothy and the Tin Man went with them.
They just flew up in a spinning tornado
Then got set back down across the road
Where they continue gathering friends
Who need hearts, brains, courage, and homes.

One can follow the yellow brick road journey
To the heart pond where Cupid's arrow hit the pink heart.
One can't miss it even if there is resistance
To this kind of growth.
Humor takes one by the heart
And tells the brain that this is art.
Home will follow you and never part
If you have the courage to follow your he/art.

Pane of Glass

Through a frosted pane of glass
Myran looks out into the dark night
Walking on cobblestone streets.
The night wears people
Of all kinds.
It has stitched them
Into the fabric of its garment
So that even after
The characters continue
Along their paths,
All who have ever
Walked in the night
Are like a trumpet player's serenade
Whose melody floats
Into a new dimension
Yet always remains.

Through a frosted pane of glass
Myran writes by candlelight
As he ponders this
And ponders that
In a collage of mystery.
The dictionary A to Z is a tool
In the medium of writing.
He places words next to words,
Mixes and pours concepts
Then surveys the contents
To discover his truth:
Be slow eternity.

Exit

Says the neon green.
From what?
Is exit really an entrance?
There is only a thin divider
Between this refined life
Of conventionality to tend to
And that which escapes definition.

When I exit
I leave my Mother Culture at the door.
Rain falls.
Colors streak down my face
Like a masquerade party.
Rain washes away my clothing.
The storm rages wild.
It breaks apart my twigs from the branches.
What's left is my skeleton.
I'm on the other side of the door, now.
Exit is a sign
That someone else may see
When they look at me.

Circus

In search
Of the circus of life
        We can cross over the threshold
                From being only human
        Into being animals varying
In character and perspective until
        We can never return
                To just being human.

        There is a horse you ride
Across the free range strands of time
        As if they belong to you
                But they do belong to you
        As long as you believe it,
As long as you don't expect
        More than life and eternity
                Can offer.

        There is a monkey
Hanging around your neck close
        To your heart.
                The river feels no longer cold.
        You squat behind its bending branches
And giggle at all you see.
        You adorn others with leaves
                And wildflowers.

        At times we find
The circus of life is figures and flesh
        Circled in acrobatic poetry.
                We beat.
        Beat palms to drums
Like rain to earth.
        We are more than just human.
                We are mad like the moon.

A Place

Streetlights sprinkle down
Through fog like rain,
Like words when only a few
Make it to paper
While others travel the hills
Out of my reach with bliss.

Was that an angel passing?

Cool night air
Infiltrates through
My cardiovascular system in a land
Famous for big rigs and gun racks,
Dogs on flatbeds
And boats tagging along.

One's out is nature
Weathering
And wilding you a little,
Keeping you just a bit more free.

There is a place
Just outside the city
Where bicycles and horses
Grip the topsoil,
Turn it over, and run free.

Over the hills
I ride the trails
To see skies of azure
With cumulus clouds.
I ride wild across the land
Galloping
With fiery free energy that says —

This Earth is mine.

I sculpt the air
And swim through oxygen molecules,
    Sometimes heavy like my blood
        When I forget I am physical;
    Sometimes dry and separated
Like my head when I forget I have one.
    I and I.
        Which?
    Sweep over tar and steel.
Together?
    Must be country road Route 1
        Perpendicular to
    Burlington Northern rail tracks.
Speed then slow.
    Rise then fall in exploration
        Of the playground.
    The journey is a route.
Engines soar along
    Rolling wheels further
        Like the little
    Caboose that thought it could.
Sometimes I just have to chant
    I think I can.
        I think I can.

Keep the Pen Moving!

When thoughts run like an athlete
Of a Red Light Green Light game,
The pen prefers to continue
Like a tractor tire spinning
In a flooded field of crops.
"Out! Out!" it cries.
The pen knows more than I
That the thought does not stop
Just because it reaches an intersection.
The engine does not stall.
The headlights do not dim.
The windshield wipers do not pause
From wiping aside
The blurring elements of misperception.
"Keep the pen moving!"
My instructors yell out
During writing exercises
To prepare us for practice
And the process that keeps us moving.
Even if no words come out,
"Keep the pen moving!"
Echoes in my memory. It ricochets,
Unlike the speeding bullets
To my father's targets.
Bull's Eye! Or rather, in between them.
"Keep the pen moving!"
Bounces off school gym ceilings
During choir rehearsal
When we sing out.
Notes brew in diaphragms and rise as gifts.
Will we falter, hesitate, stumble?
We move on regardless
Because perfecting the event
Is insignificant in the process
That keeps us moving.
"Keep the pen moving!"
Means that even if no words are formed
I must scribble or create a new language
That perhaps I have not even heard
Or that perhaps
I did not know existed but it does
Because during the moment it is created,
It becomes timeless like

The continuous reverberating motion
Of drawing the beating of a heart across a page.
The heart does not stop, but if it does
Then that is the only moment
When the pen may pause
But only the briefest pause,
Like the time it takes for another heart to beat
On its own once
Leaving the mother's womb.

Heartbeat rhythms on a page
Turn into V & V & V
Like the Dance of the Seven Veils
In which a woman named Salome
Rattles a tambourine and dances
Against the wolf mother wallpaper
Painted by a waitress named Ellen Cherry.
In *Skinny Legs and All,*
Tom Robbins creates Salome.
She whirls with wild eyes,
Drops one veil at a time
And creates visions.

Heartbeat rhythms on a page
Turn into W & W & W
Like fresh mountain Water
I drank
With an Appaloosa at my side.
We come out of hibernation and approach Spring.
In Spring, the cycles of life begin.
All the Earth renews hope of elation.
Spring showers bring April flowers.
The wind breath of Zephirus pollinates.
Crops grow in the direction of the Sun
As Earth courses around it.
Animals make their melodies.
Spiders intertwine, interlace,
Weave webs of patterns
Which have been used
Since the beginning of the species.
Small fowls such as owls
Sleep through nights
With open eye.

Heartbeat rhythms on a page
Turn into M & M & M
        Like a Magnificent Mother
                Who grew from roots of heritage
        And teaches brilliant minds.
The minds are so brilliant
        That they have not even realized
                Their brilliancy.
        We ponder on what to write
When told "Keep the pen moving!"
        As if we wish we could write better
                Or write more.

        Some gazed out the windows
Of the schoolhouse like I gazed
        Out the windows of the mobile home
                Across a green acre even then knowing
        Someday things would be better.
One may work all the day long
        Investing seed in a fertile soil
                Yet find that the riverbed has flooded
        And has washed away all.
Fields are muddy. Tractors get stuck.
        So we gaze out across a green acre
                And know that tomorrow is another day
        Or a new moon
Or a new century to celebrate.
        We continue to move on,
                To practice the process
        That keeps us moving.
Voices of a choir, rhythms of a heartbeat,
        Rooms of thinking minds,
                The twirling of Salome,
        The wolf mother wallpaper,
And spiders weaving webs make it all seem
        As if everything that exists
                Has wild eyes.

Magnetic Poetry

Question a medium
Then use the brilliant eccentric eye
To sculpt a statue allegory.
Celebrate art
As the neo-poetry self.
Melt Madonna with a fire eye
Depth of illusion.
Explore the universe
As an open graffiti canvas.
Be slow eternity
Cranking a ferocious circle
In a 20th century night
That births ghosts.
Is it a blue hue period?
Can words cloud up my sky?
I laugh and rage poetry.

Listen . . .
Growl . . .
We want
Roasted coffee beans.
Brew strong espresso aroma.
Pour life calmly.
Coffee is breakfast.
Drink its vital flavor.
Wake with hot power
To sacred mornings.
Etch a full and fresh
Lingering
Smile.

Good Morning!

I hope you slept well. Waking up takes time.
Have the gods been playing with your mind?
Have you had dreams of shadow people
Surrounding you in theater?

An old green van has a flat tire
On your trip through the country where old barns
Speckle across land so everyone threw
Up their hands.
A tire is a continuous circle
With no beginning and no end like the preacher says
Of your wedding rings but your trip went flat
And even your road rage subsided.

You there, quiet one,
Why do you look so far off into the distance?
Do you have a secret?
Do you have a dream?
Why are you waiting?
A man and girl child wait also.
Do they reside in your inner psyche?
A school bus offers to pick you up
To take you where they go.
A motorcyclist stops to chat
But you stay and wait
For something else.

Hey, look! The tire is fixed.
Once again, there is no beginning or end.
It waits to spin its cycle like a marriage
Should do after counseling.
The license plate was also replaced
You notice as everyone piles in. Numbers and letters
Represent identity and something here changed.
There is no room for you only because
You ask no one to slide over.
Instead, you remain in the country a while.
If there is a time for everything
Then this is the time for change.

Eucalyptus

Is the scent I scented my candles with.
Jello red shaped like stars,
        Votives, pyramids, and shapes of
                Restroom little girl and boy.

Tomorrow I will drive
To another home of mine and take
        Mother some eucalyptus
                Left after a wedding reception
        In the banquet hall of the beach resort.
During dinner on my birthday I will tell her
        About some of the funny characters
                I met where I work.
        I'm sure I will tell her
About the comment card that read
        "You should sell little Christa dolls
                So everywhere I eat
        I will be reminded
Of excellent customer service."
        I know most certainly that I will tell her
                Of the lady who called
        To hear about our prices and view,
Menu and salads and if it is a nice place.
        After consulting with her husband,
                She decided to make reservations.
        I asked for how many people and she replied
"Two, unless I bring my multiple personalities
        In which case there will only be one since
                My husband can't stand any of them."

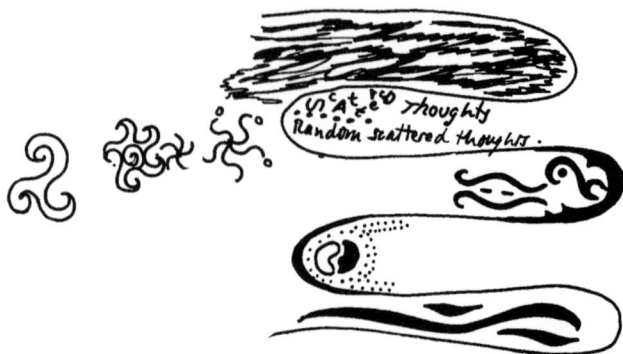

104

Bones

I stare at you—
    Staring . . .
        Staring . . .
My gaze studies you—
    You and your bones
        In functional places.
Students draw
    Standing at easels
        Me and my bones.
They apologize for the nose
    Say it is the hardest part
        Though it's made of cartilage.
You have no nose—
    You skeleton poster
        I stare at for lengths.
I am quiet and still—
    A naked mannequin
        Performing duty.
I hold pose for artists
    On a raised platform
        In the center of a room.
Each of their newsprint sheets
    Displays expressions
        Of thoughts or emotions.
Yet I just stand here
    Staring at your bones
        Against paper.
Back in the skull
    Memory trickles
        Down the spine.
Vertebra by vertebra
    Like rain on windows
        Everything is clear.
We remember with our bones
    So when I rest and wither
        I will leave my bones.

Letter

If I were to write you a letter
I would tell you that each morning is new
    And does not copy the former
Coastal fog surrounding you.

    A flat-topped rock is a chair
And ocean waves are music
    In symphony. Every organism is a player
And my part is writing words becoming lyric.

    How I got here was a wooden staircase
With a few steps missing on the descent
    So with instinct I slowed pace
Because slipping might be my end.

    Only when waves are of good size
Are there surfers that swim this far.
    Today's flat sea means solitude is my prize
Except for insects landing on my paper.

    Alone I watch starfish gripping rock
Or sea birds in their patterns left and right
    Much more graceful than my tennis luck
Because my performance is a funny sight.

    Tonight my friends will have a bonfire
With earth sea air fire and the full moon.
    We are on the beach as September ends summer
And many who are here will make their move.

    I will not be lonely, though, in my beautiful garden
With time to write and cats for company.
    My Calico India explores her own forest glen
While I make soups and candles and find things to study.

Scratching the Surface

You're just scratching the surface
She says
Working a bit at this
And a bit at that,
Have so many options
And opportunities.

You're just scratching the surface
She says
Putting energy fully
Into one activity or two
For a while until realizing
A new path you were meant to take.

You're just scratching the surface
She says
Of understanding who you are
Like a fragment of your being
Like a fragment
Of your potential.

You're just scratching the surface
She says
With edges that might cut
With edges you didn't know you had
With edges you back away from
And edges that tickle like the Sun.

You're just scratching the surface
She says
Of all the places you want to go
As if there awaits that world
That will give a bit of all your favorites
So that you can give it all away.

Peter Iredale

I travel
While listening to Suzanne Vega
Reverberate wisdom like a pebble
Skipping across water.
She sings about "Night Vision"
From her sound box.

I look
For the *Peter Iredale* shipwreck
And turn at the sign
"Historical Marker."
The paved road
Becomes a packed road of dirt,
Rocks and roots.
There are a few roots in the road.
There are a few routes in the road.

I park
At the fork in the road.
Down one way
I find roots
Of words on my route
Like ancestry trickling
Down my spinal cord.
Down the other way
I see the sea.
When I reach the ocean shore
Where water, earth, and air meet,
I feel fire in my center
Because I know
Peter Iredale is there.
It is just a bit farther down the beach.

Click. Click.
I take
A pair of photos
Of this ship wrecked in October 1906
Where it rests and erodes
Its way through time
With the salt of the sea.

The journey
Felt more significant
Than the destination.

Character Cake

On the morning of my birthday
I dreamt of waking to wrinkles
Around my eyes.
Mother said it meant
I gained a little wisdom.
We both gained a little humor
When we saw that black spider cake—
Two white eyes,
Blood red zig-zag mouth, and
Black fury frosting. It was called Character Cake.
The baker had a lot of character
To make that cake
So that we could
Stand side by side
And laugh at the spider
We would eat that night.

Halloween

I am the concept of Halloween.
I am a day that someone else experiences.
I am finished with this
Book because it is
Time to share it
With you
As I
Melt
Away.

I fill in the pages
Of a spiral notebook
Like days that God gives to me
And wants me to share
With you who may be hurting
But trying to heal
So go to the place
That tonight is the Bat-room
To relieve yourself.

I prepare the day
With exercise and with fasting
Because I am hungry for something else
That I get when oxygen in the body
Does not need to break down food
And can therefore be free
To move into the head
So I think and feel
All the more alive.

Strength
Stability Mobility
How I looked at those words
This morning on the gym wall
And wished I could
Write them so they
Might sound
Poetic.

I keep writing
In this notebook
Like it's the best thing I've ever done
And I wonder when my guests show up
Will they think I'm crazy
But then I remember
My invitations read
Dusk
And we are all coming
As our Halloween madness
Masquerading as we choose
Knowing that life is not planned
By mortals
Because the gods are in control
And we have to keep laughing
Spontaneously
And not let
The ghouls get us down.

I throw a party
To share this madness
But you have to be willing to fight
To stay alive
And you have to be brave
To share
And you have to be a bit selfish
To say
"This time is mine.
This is my life.
I make her story."

I have to have
Gone somewhere
Before I can come back to you
With wild eyes
Before I can welcome you
Through a Hermann Hesse door
And say
"Leave Your Mind At The Door
Mad Persons Welcome"
Before I can have a party
And like Anaïs Nin write
"Come As Your Madness."

"I am as blank as paper
And as full as night."
That's what I said once
When someone asked my age.
That's what I am today
With a notebook decorated
With duct and electrical tape.
This body wears a black cape
Another body once wore
To *Phantom of the Opera.*
In my ears, the kokopelli flute player
Tells stories through music.
Exira, the wooden snake
Announced herself on the beach one day
Standing out from the driftwood and now
Slithers around my neck
Hissing.

I pin the cover
Of my story on the wall
And stand to look at the silhouette.
She steps
Moving heels
Like question marks
And I follow
Because I completed
This wave of time.
I must move
To keep the air clear
And to remember
This as a beautiful place
That I will miss.

I must take this moment
NOW
Forever on my way
Because tomorrow,
If it ever gets here,
May be a battle.
We just have to believe.
We have to really believe
That it makes a difference
And know
That all we have given
Does not go unnoticed.
It is multiplied into the world.

I follow the signs
Like question marks
To find out where they go.
That is why I put a question mark
Around the address.
On this evening
People will ask where Halloween is.
When they see the question mark
Around my address
They will know.

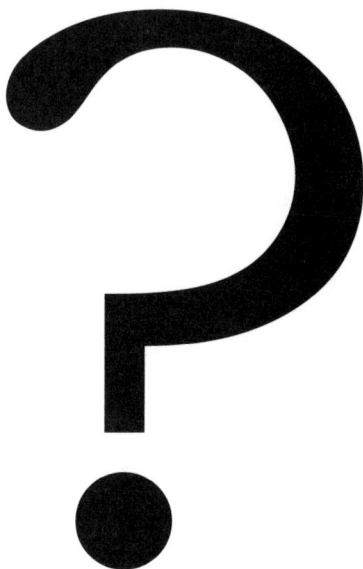

Puzzle: Piece 1

Another word on another page
And God said "So Be It"
So you may as well, if you are anything,
Be whatever you believe
It is.

The objective might be to present an aria,
A song composed of three parts
As defined by the 1896
Dictionary of Musical Terms.
Or the objective might be another form of
Mythology playing itself out
In a modern day story.

Scribble.
Make your mark.
Don't wait for perfection.
You will wait forever.
Don't wait for someone else
To identify the model as art.
She doesn't wait
To become art
Until you see her as that.
She is who she is.
Maybe what you paint
Is more a reflection of yourself.

What is the missing piece of puzzle?
It is the reflection of life.
It is the merging of energies.
It is the filling of the pages
As they turn on the spiral.

It is those spaces,
Aria said during yoga,
That open up the mind
And work out the toxicity.
Stretch the spinal cord
Vertebra
One by one.

One by one or step by step
Toward a whole vision.

Gamut versus Morpheus.
You can't have one without the other.

And Gamut said
"Without my baby steps
Life is just a vision unexperienced.
I am the scale and the spectrum."

And Morpheus said
"Without my vision of the whole
Life is just baby steps fragmented
Into multiple directions
With no true destination."

And so it came to pass
That Gamut and Morpheus
Agreed to join together
To fit individual puzzle pieces
Into one great masterpiece.

Puzzle: Piece II

As a child
I made a puzzle in art class
Of spirals back and forth
Across the page.
I wove lines
To fill in spaces.
Every puzzle piece of the whole
Had spirals and spaces.
It was black and white
Like my mother's piano keys.
When I put the puzzle together
It just spiraled
Across the page like my pen.

Lines run through my head
Like a collage of fabrics
Colored like a road map
Held together with a single safety pin.
A safety pen puts it all on paper
Before my brain
Forgets what it is doing.
Each thread is a rhythm of music
Moving through me
If only because I can't stop it.

Red means stop.
Green means go.
Maybe I should write those directions
On the back of my thumb
Like it was suggested
During the introduction
To the street signal.

When I put the notebook
On my lap while driving
Lines ride through my head.
I write on half the page
As I drive on half the road
Of asphalt painted by dashed white
On which I travel to Mount Saint Helens
With a friend where I will
Eventually have a dream.

Puzzle: Piece III

We gather in a circle in this dream
Where candles flicker like stars.
There is a little light
For us to see shadows on the cave wall
So that we can make up stories
About what we are doing here.

We sit in lotus
Resembling the white flower
That grows from mud.
We meditate
On letters and words
Placed in the center
Of the concentric circle.
They all stem from the root words
Ubi and Ibi.

Ubiquitous
Means everywhere.

Ibidem
Repeats itself.

In a footnote ibidem means
The same author as quoted before.
There is only one set of footprints
Making marks
Traveling in time
Between land and sea
With words of divinity
With words of infinity.

Echo verse is a language
Which I use for play—
Echo . . .
Echo . . .
Echo . . .
Reverberation
Like the sound spirals make
Once the circle
Of infinity is complete.
Divinity
Echo

One plays solitaire.
Two is a pair
Like two wings of a bird
Or two parts of a story
Where Aria dreamt language
And I dreamt form.
When the wings come together
They flap out a story.

And there is a person in my dream
Who is a part of the circle of friends
Sitting in lotus.
After we meditated
On the words in the center
And transcended
Our prior reality,
He thanked me and offered a gift
In exchange
But I told him
That my reward was watching him
Experience this
As my reader.